Wake

Sleepy I

EARLY MORNIN

Mand

illustrated by
Dubravka Kolanovic

Published by Child's Play (International) Ltd
Swindon   Auburn ME   Sydney
Text © 2004 M. Ross   Illustrations © 2004 Child's Play (International) Ltd   All rights reserved
ISBN 1-904550-33-9   www.childs-play.com   Printed in Croatia
1 3 5 7 9 10 8 6 4 2

Warthog

I'm a little warthog.
I like to wake up early
To wash my fur in dewdrops,
And keep it nice and curly.

skunk

Sleeping sound, stinking sweet,
My little skunkadee.
Such a shame to wake you,
My little stinkaree.

Don't wash, my darling!
My little pongaroo.
We love you when your pong's strong,
My little honkydoo.

Sweet day, scented day,
My little odouriffy.
Every day's a smelly day,
My little whiffysniffy.

Rhinoceros

Wake up, my little rhino!
Oh, pretty baby mine-o!
Your dainty ears, your baby horn,
Your darling face lights up the dawn,
More beautiful than any other –
No one loves you like your mother.

Koala

High up a gum tree,
We babies hold tight,
From night until morning,
And morning till night.
A baby koala
Holds onto its mum,
'Cause nothing is snugger
Than mum up a gum.

Cow and calf

Moooo!
Good morning to yoooou!
The sky is bluuuue,
And cooool is the dewwww.
There's grass to chewwww,
So wake up, doooo!
Moooo!

Pig

I dream of breakfast
All through the night...
And every morning,
To my delight,
As day dawns
My dream comes true!
A bucket of slops –
May it happen to you!

Horse

Dandelions? Daisies?
Buttercups? Clover?
Or meadowsweet for breakfast,
Now the night's over?

Panda

Bamboo for breakfast,
Bamboo for lunch.
Bamboo for supper,
Munch! Munch! Munch!

Puffin

Down below the dawn
And down below the waves,
Breakfast was swimming with a swish, swish, swish.

High in the sky
And high on the cliffs,
Breakfast comes flying – here's your fish, fish, fish.

Jellyfish

Jellyfish dreaming,
Tentacles streaming,
Sunlight beaming,
Deep-sea dreaming.
Asleep, awake,
We go with the flow.
Where will the tides take us today?
Over the ocean and far away.

Crab

Nip! Nip! Nip!
Good morning, little nipper.
Time to stretch your shell.
There's small fry for breakfast,
Tide's turning, all's well.

Snake

Breakfasssst, little ssssquiggler.
Sssssstretch those jawsssss open wide…
No, come on, wider… wider ssssstill!
Let'ssss sssseee what you can fit insssside.

Anteater

Good morning, little anteater.
What will you eat for breakfast today?
Cornflakes? Porridge? Bacon and eggs?
Just ants? As usual? Oh. Okay.

Peacock

What is the use
Of darkness at night
When your tail is beautiful?
Oh! Bring on the light!

Zebra

Under the marvellous magical moon
We're midnight blue and silver bright,
Until the morning, when we wake –
Just plain old zebras, black and white.

Chameleon

Midnight-blue pyjamas,
The same every night.
We long for the dawn,
For colour and light.

When daybreak comes,
Whether warm or cold,
We dress for the sunrise
In purple and pink, with streaks of gold.

Seal

Aark! Aark!
Aark! Aark!

When you've no arms or legs,
And your flippers are tiny,
It's a wearisome wriggle
Into the briny…

SPLOSH!

But under the water, we're streaming and swooping,
Dancing and turning and gliding and looping,
Through forests of seaweed, we chase and we race,
Streamlined and silky in seawater grace.

sloth

Is it morning? Hear us snore.
We stretch, turn over, sleep some more.
Is it morning? The jungle stirs.
The leopards, monkeys, frogs and birds
Are busy peeping, creeping, leaping.
We're busy too. (We're busy sleeping!)

Elephants

Trumpety trump!
Good morning, herd!
Time for our jumbo exercises.
Ready? And…

Four steps left and four steps right,
Every morning and every night.
Trunks up high and trunks down low,
Turn to the left and round we go.

Kneel to the front and kneel to the rear.
Wiggle your tail and waggle each ear.
Now jump! jump! jump!
With a thump! thump! thump!
And welcome the day
With a trumpety trump!

Spider

Good morning, my babies.
This morning, it's time for your
Very first spinning lesson.

First, choose a corner,
A room with a view.
A hedge, or a flower,
A place just for you.

Now start your spinning,
Threads silky and strong.
Don't get them tangled
Or spin them too long.

Start at the corners
And work your way in,
Round and around
In a slow, careful spin.

Your first web! It's a beauty!
You can try it for size.
Now, catch your own breakfast –
Some nice, crispy flies!

Kangaroo

BOING! BOING! BOING!
BOING! BOING! BOING!
We leap in the morning
When the day has begun,
And we leap all day
In the baking hot sun.
BOING! BOING! BOING!
BOING! BOING! BOING!

Joey

BOING! BOING! BOING!
BOING! BOING! BOING!
In my snug pouch-pocket,
I spend the day sleeping,
And I leap in my dreams
As my mum goes leaping.
BOING! BOING! BOING!
BOING! BOING! BOING!

Monkey

Hee! Hee! Hee!
Good morning to me!
Hoo! Hoo! Hoo!
Good morning to you!
Scratch! Scratch! Scratch!
Find those fleas!
Now eat your banana
And swing in the trees.

B e e

Morning!
Sunrise!
Find a flower…
And fertilise!

Buzzing in and out the flowers,
Dancing in between the showers,
Each tiny pollen-dust collector,
Busy bringing home the nectar,
Working all the hours it's sunny,
Busy, buzzy, making honey.

Dog

Sniff the morning
And sniff the dawn.
Scratch all over
And stretch and yawn.

Prick up your ears...
Footsteps, humming.
Race to meet them –
At last, they're coming!

Fetch your leash
And sniff out the keys.
Beg for a walk!
Let's go! Now! Please!

Cockerel

COCK-A-DOODLE DOO!
Bock! Bock! Bock!
Chuck! Chuck! Chuck!
Peck? Peck? Peck?
Cluck! Cluck! Cluck!
COCK-A-DOODLE DOO!

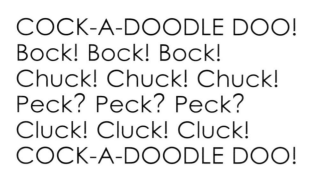

Translation:

CALLING ALL CHICKS AND CHUCKS!

Out of the henhouse and into the day.
Too early? Certainly not! Dear, dear! I should say!
My dear Madam, tell me, have you laid your egg today?
And you, Madam? Nor you, Madam?
Dear, dear, dear! To your laying stations!
My dear ladies! It's time to lay!

NOT A MOMENT TO LOSE! CHOCKS AWAY!

Cat

During the night,
I'm a yowling, prowling, catch-a-mouse cat.

But when it's light,
I turn into a furry, purry, come-into-the-house cat,
A rub-against-your-legs cat,
Is-breakfast-ready-yet cat,
A milk-and-cream, sleep-and-dream
Till night-is-bright-again cat.

Owl

Whoo-whoo-whoo!
When the morning
Grows blue-whoo-whoo,
It's 'Good night' for us,
And 'Good morning'
For you-whoo-whoo.

Hedgehog

Sniff… sniff… sniff…
Snuffle… snuffle… snuffle…
Morning…
Dawning…
Yawning…
Pile of leaves…
Shuffle… shuffle… shuffle….
Creeping…
Peeping…
Rustle… rustle… rustle...
Sleeping.

Bird

We don't need pyjamas.
Feathers are best
For snuggling down
In a comfortable nest.

We don't need alarm clocks.
We've no trouble waking.
We sing our dawn chorus,
As daylight is breaking.

slug

Good morning, fellow slugs,
It's a sluggish sort of day.
The rain is raining nicely
So we'll slither on our way.

Snail

Take a peep
Outside your shell.
Tentacles first,
Then body as well.

Watery-wet,
The garden is dawning.
It's drippy! We're happy!
The best kind of morning!

Rabbit

Earth brown,
Sky blue,
Grass green,
Fresh dew.
Early start,
Clean habits.
Out of the burrow,
Little rabbits!

Frog

In the morning it's cool
Beside our pool.
And if the day grows hot,
A frog need not!
SPLOSH!

Human

Good morning, little sleepyhead,
Warm and snug inside your bed.
Cock-a-doodle! Dawn is breaking,
All the animals are waking.

The elephants are exercising,
Fish are swimming in the seas.
The cows are eating breakfast,
The monkeys catching fleas.

The kangaroos are bouncing,
(Though the sloths are still in bed.)
The day's begun, my little one,
So wake up, sleepyhead!